Thomas the Rhymer

RETOLD BY JUDY PATERSON

ILLUSTRATED BY SALLY J. COLLINS

THE AMAISING PUBLISHING HOUSE LTD

DEDICATION
To Sheila
A true friend is the best possession

ACKNOWLEDGEMENTS
From the poem, Thomas The Rhymer, a traditional
ballad of the 13th Century.
My thanks to Sheila Maher and Aileen Paterson
for advice and encouragement.

GLOSSARY
WORDS IN ORDER AS THEY APPEAR IN TEXT

laird	a noble lord
tower house	a small fortess-house
broom	a yellow flowering gorse bush
burn	a small stream
brownies	fairy folk who sometimes help in the house at night

Text © Judy Paterson
Illustrations © Sally J. Collins

Published in 1998 by
The Amaising Publishing House Ltd. Unit 7, Greendykes Industrial Estate,
Broxburn, West Lothian, EH52 6PG, Scotland

Telephone 01506-857570
Fax 01506-858100

ISBN 1 871512 60 3

Printed and bound by Scotprint Ltd, Musselburgh

Page layout by Mark Blackadder

Reprint Code   10   9   8   7   6   5   4   3   2   1

In the Borders of Scotland, a long long time ago, there lived a young man called Thomas. Thomas was a Laird and lived in a strong Tower House. He was the lord of all the beautiful lands close by and he was a very happy man. Thomas liked to make rhymes and to play music.

One day, while Thomas was walking in the woods he heard the sound of singing and the tinkling of little bells.

Through the trees he saw a beautiful lady riding a dapple grey horse.

She was dressed in the greens of the forest and her long hair was the colour of corn. She wore a crown of gold sparkling with emeralds and rubies. There were more jewels on her fingers and her horse had golden reins jingling with tiny bells. Thomas took off his hat and bowed very low.

"Welcome to my lands, fair lady," said Thomas. "Who are you?"

"I am the Queen of a far-away land," laughed the beautiful lady. "Have you a kiss for the Queen of Fairyland?"

Thomas could not help falling under her spell. He closed his eyes and gave her a kiss but her lips felt like ice! Thomas stepped back in surprise. The beautiful Queen had gone and before him stood an ancient old lady! The forest green clothes had changed to rags of grey cobwebs. The golden hair was now silvery white and framed a face deeply lined with time. Only the bright eyes still laughed.

"Your fairy kiss has cost you seven years, Thomas. For seven years you shall be my servant."

Thomas shook his head. He had been tricked. "Please forgive me," he begged. "I have my family and my lands to look after."

The old lady crooked a long horny finger at him, "Come Thomas, ride with me to Fairyland. You cannot refuse this Queen and I have chosen you because we fairies love the music of the Borders. You shall play for us."

Thomas was very frightened but he climbed onto the back of the strong horse.

For a long time Thomas rode behind the Queen of Fairyland. Eventually, they came to a halt on the edge of a bleak moor and the Queen spoke softly.

"There are only three roads in life Thomas, but few mortals see them. Look carefully now." she said and the moorland melted before his eyes as she pointed a long bony finger.

"That is an easy road, but if you chose that road through life you would come to a bad end." Her long finger moved towards a hidden, twisted and steep pathway through briars and brambles. "Very few men take that path. It needs a strong heart and hard work to travel that long and weary way. It leads to peace and happiness."

"And the third road?" Thomas asked. He looked at the gentle pathway leading between the bracken and the yellow of the broom.

The old lady sighed happily, "That, my dear Thomas, is a road few mortals can walk for it leads to Fairyland. That is our road, the road to Fairyland."

Thomas looked behind him sadly
but his home was far, far away.

"Thomas," said the old Queen kindly, "listen carefully if
you want to see your home and family again. For seven years
you will serve me in Fairyland and for seven years you must not speak.
Remember, one word from your lips will make you my servant forever."

Thomas shut his lips tight as they set off down the road to Fairyland.

It was a long journey and the road became narrower and narrower as they
went deeper and deeper into a ravine. Soon it was so dark Thomas could not see.
He could smell the damp and woody earth, and he could hear the running
of water in little burns. He felt the branches of the trees catching at his
clothes as they passed.

At last, after many hours, the sun appeared. All around were beautiful fruit trees and Thomas smelt the warm ripe pears, apples and cherries. The grass was wet with dew and he saw bright red strawberries. He longed for something to eat.

The haggard old lady spoke to him, "While you are in Fairyland Thomas, you must eat nothing except the apple I will give to you. If you eat anything else you will be poisoned and you will remain in Fairyland forever."

The old woman reached into the branches of a small tree bursting with glossy red apples. She picked just one. "These are the Apples of Truth. Once you have eaten this, Thomas, no lie will pass from your lips."

The Queen pointed to a hillside where a dazzling castle gleamed in the sunlight. Its tall towers reached up into the blue sky. "There is my home," she smiled. She pulled out her hunting horn and blew so loud and strong that Thomas wondered how an old lady had so much breath.

Suddenly the horse reared up and Thomas fell to the ground. When he got to his feet, he was so surprised that he clamped his hand over his mouth for fear of speaking out loud. There sitting on the proud grey horse was the beautiful maiden, dressed again in her greens and her fine jewellery!

She smiled at him, "Thomas, you are now my page-boy, and remember," she said, "not one word. Here come the folk of Fairyland to welcome us."

There were pixies and elves and fairies with fine silver wings. They were dressed in the petals of flowers and they skipped and hopped and cheered as Thomas led the Fairy Queen along the road up to the castle.

They all trooped into the main hall where the King sat on his tall throne. Before she sat down on her own throne, the Queen gave Thomas a small harp.

"I will call you to play for my Lord the King," she said. "We love the music from your world."

Thomas bowed and found himself a seat where he was out of the way. As he tuned the harp he watched.

There was a great deal of noise and people were running too and fro. Servants set up long tables for a great feast. Cooks brought in roasted meats and enormous pies. Kitchen maids carried golden jugs of wine and towering baskets of fruits.

All the time Thomas watched and kept his lips firmly closed. He took none of the fine food and nothing to drink.

The feasting went on through the night. There was singing and dancing and Thomas clapped his hands and tapped his feet. It seemed as if no-one wanted to sleep.

There were elves who juggled precious gems and brownies who raced on the backs of rabbits. Little fairy children ran in and out playing chasing games with huge dogs between the tables and chairs. Thomas thought it was all wonderful.

"Won't you have some strawberries?" asked one little girl.

"Won't you tell us your name?" teased a small boy.

Thomas smiled at them but he remembered to eat no food and to say not one word.

At last the Queen called to Thomas. He passed through the crowd with his harp and sat at the feet of the Queen. He played the soft haunting songs of his homeland. The great hall grew quiet.

Thomas played until the first rays of the sun crept over the edge of the earth. Now almost everyone had fallen asleep.

"Come Thomas!" said the Queen, "You have done well and now you can return to your Tower House."

Thomas was amazed and almost spoke but he remembered the warning just in time and shut his lips tight. "This must be a trick!" he thought. "I have not been here for seven years."

"You do well to remember your silence Thomas," laughed the Queen, "but truly you have been here for seven years. However, if you would like to stay forever you only need to ask me."

Thomas looked round the lovely hall and then at the beautiful Fairy Queen and he shook his head. No matter how wonderful it was, he could not stay. It was time to return to his family.

Once again Thomas rode on the grey
horse behind the Fairy Queen. Before any time
at all he was home on the edge of the woods.

When Thomas slipped down from the horse he
cleared his throat. It was strange to hear his own voice
after such a long silence.

"Thank you for the gift of Truth My Lady, but may
I have a small token to remember my visit to Fairyland."

The Fairy Queen smiled, "I shall give you the gift of
rhyming so that you may write poems and I shall give you
the gift of prophesy so you may foretell the future. You shall
be known as True Thomas for your truth, and as Thomas the
Rhymer for your poems. For your prophecies you will be
remembered for all time."

"Thank you," he said. "These are wonderful gifts, but will
I ever see you again?"

She smiled and from her saddle-bag she took a
beautifully carved harp. It was decorated with gold and
inset with mother of pearl and brightly coloured enamels.

"Think of me when you play, Thomas. One day I shall
send for you."

When Thomas walked into his own great hall his poor family had such a shock. His wife ran to him, "Thomas! We have waited for seven long years! Where have you been?"

Thomas shook his head. He could not say he had been to Fairyland but he could not tell a lie. "I have been travelling far away and I have learned many things," he said.

He looked at his children,

"You have grown so much." Seven years really had passed. He felt sad.

"Father! What a beautiful harp!" said the youngest child when she saw the wonderful instrument. "Where did it come from? Play for me."

Thomas smiled and sat by the fire with his family. He played soft tunes on the fairy harp.

As time passed people forgot how Thomas had disappeared for seven long years. They often admired the beautiful harp but Thomas never told them it came from Fairyland.

One night Thomas dreamt about a terrible storm. He saw the King riding through the wind and rain and he saw an accident. Thomas knew this was the fairy gift of prophecy.

On March 19 in 1286, King Alexander 111 rode from Edinburgh and crossed the Forth. The King rode through a storm but his horse stumbled and he fell to his death over the cliffs at Kinghorn.

People remembered that Thomas had foretold the King's death. He became known as a wise man and folk came to him for advice when they had problems. Thomas always told them the truth.

The Rhymes and Prophesies of Thomas were often curious because they told about things that would happen in the future. People began to believe his gift of seeing into the future must have come from Fairyland.

Thomas was a very old man by this time, and though he never spoke of it, he had never forgotten his visit to the fairy world.

One moonlit night, the guards on the tower saw a strange sight. Two white deer, a hart and a hind, were making their way through the trees in the parklands. They stood and waited close by the great gates.

"I've never seen white deer before," muttered one of the men.

"It must be an omen," said the other. "We must tell Thomas."

Old Thomas smiled when he heard the news. "At last the messengers have come from Fairyland. I must go."

H e picked up his harp and went into the moonlit garden.
The snow-white deer waited for him and led Thomas into the
woods, through the trees and across the little river. They were never
seen again.

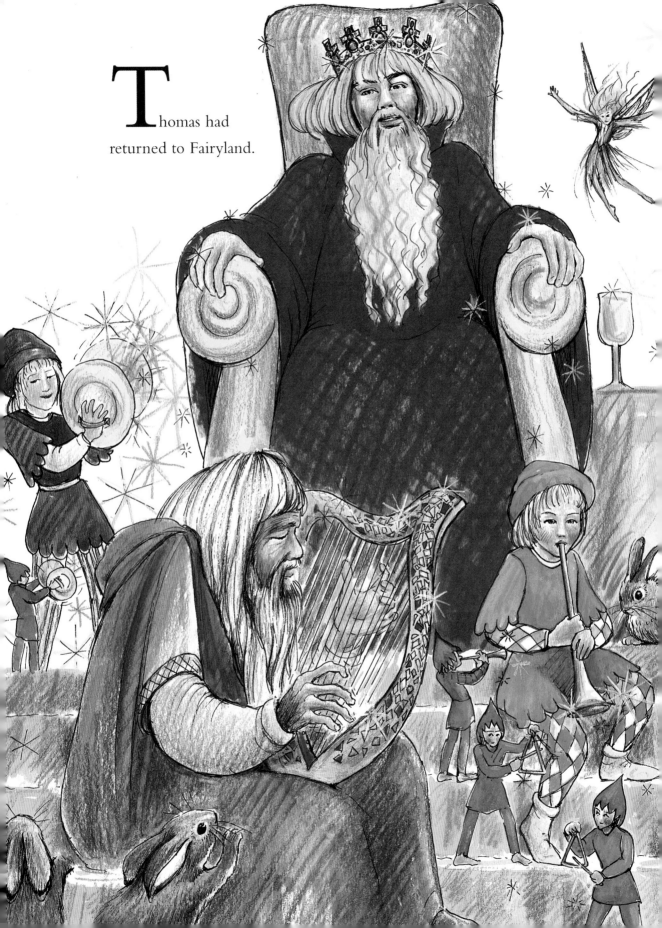

Thomas had returned to Fairyland.

Thomas of Erceldoune was a real man, a laird in the borders of Scotland. Erceldoune, in Berwickshire, was the site of a town and the castle of the Earl of Dunbar and March. Today it is known as Earlston which is near Melrose. Thomas owned lands and a "tower" of his own. He lived approximately between 1210 and 1290.

He was a poet with a reputation as a seer, or soothsayer. He lived at the time when Wallace was leading the Scots against King Edward of England, the Hammer of the Scots.

It is not really known how many of Thomas's "predictions" were truly his. As time went by Thomas became a legend and storytellers added to the "predictions", maybe even after the historical events took place.

One rhyme foretold the Battle of Bannockburn in 1314 when Robert the Bruce defeated the English:

The Burn of Breid   *The Burn of Bread...(bannock)*
Shall rin fou reid.   *Shall run full red...(with blood)*

Another rhyme predicted the day when Britain was ruled by one king :-

A French Queen shall bearre the Sonne;
Shall rule all Britainne to the sea,
As neere as in the ninth degree

This happened in 1603, when James, son of Mary Queen of Scots who had been a French Queen, was crowned King of both Scotland and England. He was ninth in line to the English throne.

Thomas also saw the day when the Highlands would be cleared of their clans and crofters to make way for sheep.

The teeth of the sheep shall lay the plough on the shelf.